It's tir...
COWS...

Genius cow Professor McMoo and his
trusty sidekicks, Pat and Bo, are star
agents of the C.I.A. – short for
COWS IN ACTION!
They travel through time, fighting evil
bulls from the future and keeping
history on the right track . . .

Find out more at
www.cowsinaction.com

READ MORE STEVE COLE BOOKS!

ASTROSAURS

Riddle of the Raptors
The Hatching Horror
The Seas of Doom
The Mind-Swap Menace
The Skies of Fear
The Space Ghosts
Day of the Dino-Droids
The Terror-Bird Trap
The Planet of Peril
The Star Pirates
The Claws of Christmas

The Sun-Snatchers
Revenge of the FANG
The Carnivore Curse
The Dreams of Dread
The Robot Raiders
The Twist of Time
The Sabre-Tooth Secret
The Forest of Evil
The T.rex Invasion
The Castle of Frankensaur

ASTROSAURS ACADEMY

Destination: Danger!
Contest Carnage!
Terror Underground!
Jungle Horror!

Deadly Drama!
Christmas Crisis!
Volcano Invaders!
Space Kidnap!

COWS IN ACTION

The Ter-moo-nators
The Moo-my's Curse
The Roman Moo-stery
The Wild West Moo-nster
World War Moo
The Battle for Christmoos
The Pirate Moo-tiny

The Moo-gic of Merlin
The Victorian Moo-ders
The Moo-lympic Games
First Cows on the Mooon
The Udderly Moovellous
Joke Book

SLIME SQUAD

The Slime Squad Vs The Fearsome Fists
The Slime Squad Vs The Toxic Teeth
The Slime Squad Vs The Cyber-Poos
The Slime Squad Vs The Supernatural Squid
The Slime Squad Vs The Killer Socks
The Slime Squad Vs The Last-Chance Chicken
The Slime Squad Vs The Alligator Army
The Slime Squad Vs The Conquering Conks

THE WILD WEST MOO-NSTER

Steve Cole

Illustrated by Woody Fox

RED FOX

THE WILD WEST MOO-NSTER
A RED FOX BOOK 978 1 862 30192 4

First published in Great Britain by Red Fox,
an imprint of Random House Children's Publishers UK
A Random House Group Company

This edition published 2008

5 7 9 10 8 6 4

Set in Bembo Schoolbook

Red Fox Books are published by Random House Children's Publishers UK,
61–63 Uxbridge Road, London W5 5SA

www.**randomhousechildrens**.co.uk
www.randomhouse.co.uk
Addresses for companies within
The Random House Group Limited can be found at:
www.randomhouse.co.uk/offices.htm

THE RANDOM HOUSE GROUP Limited Reg. No. 954009

A CIP catalogue record for this book is available from the British Library.

Printed in the UK by
Clays Ltd, St Ives plc

For Tom Whone

★ THE C.I.A. FILES ★

Cows from the present —
Fighting in the past to protect the future . . .

In the year 2550, after thousands of years of being eaten and milked, cows finally live as equals with humans in their own country of Luckyburger. But a group of evil war-loving bulls — the Fed-up Bull Institute — is not satisfied.

Using time machines and deadly ter-moo-nator agents, the F.B.I. is trying to change Earth's history. These bulls plan to enslave all humans and put savage cows in charge of the planet. Their actions threaten to plunge all cowkind into cruel and cowardly chaos . . .

The C.I.A. was set up to stop them.

However, the best agents come not from 2550 — but from the present. From a time in the early 21st century, when the first clever cows began to appear. A time when a brainy bull named Angus McMoo invented the first time machine, little realizing he would soon become the F.B.I.'s number one enemy . . .

COWS OF COURAGE —
TOP SECRET FILES

PROFESSOR ANGUS MCMOO
Security rating: Bravo Moo Zero
Stand-out features: Large white squares on coat, outstanding horns
Character: Scatterbrained, inventive, plucky and keen
Likes: Hot tea, history books, gadgets
Hates: Injustice, suffering, poor-quality tea bags
Ambition: To invent the electric sundial

LITTLE BO VINE

Security rating: For your cow pies only

Stand-out features: Luminous udder (colour varies)

Character: Tough, cheeky, ready-for-anything rebel

Likes: Fashion, chewing gum, self-defence classes

Hates: Bessie Barmer: the farmer's wife

Ambition: To run her own martial arts club for farmyard animals

PAT VINE

Security rating: Licence to fill (stomach with grass)

Stand-out features: Zigzags on coat

Character: Brave, loyal and practical

Likes: Solving problems, anything Professor McMoo does

Hates: Flies not easily swished by his tail

Ambition: To find a five-leaf clover — and to survive his dangerous missions!

Prof. McMoo's TIMELINE OF NOTABLE HISTORICAL EVENTS

13.7 billion years BC ★
BIG BANG – UNIVERSE BEGINS
(and first tea atoms created)

4.6 billion years BC ★
PLANET EARTH FORMS
(good job too)

23 million years BC ★
FIRST COWS APPEAR
(23 million is my lucky number!)

1700 BC
SHEN NUNG MAKES FIRST CUP OF TEA
(what a hero!)

7000 BC ★
FIRST CATTLE KEPT ON FARMS
(Not a great year for cows)

1901 AD
QUEEN VICTORIA DIES
(she was not a-moo-sed)

★ (by an Egyptian geezer)

2550 BC
GREAT PYRAMID BUILT AT GIZA

31 BC
ROMAN EMPIRE FOUNDED

(Roam-Moo empire founded by a cow but no one remembers that)

1509 AD
HENRY VIII COMES TO THE THRONE

(and probably squashes it)

1066 AD
BATTLE OF HASTINGS

(but what about the Cattle of Hastings?)

1620 AD
ENGLISH PILGRIMS SETTLE IN AMERICA

(bringing with them the first cows to moo in an American accent)

1939 AD
WORLD WAR TWO BEGINS

(or World War Moo as it is known to cows)

2007 AD
I INVENT A TIME MACHINE!!!

2500 AD
COW NATION OF LUCKYBURGER FOUNDED

(HOORAY!)

2550 AD
COWS IN ACTION RECRUIT PROFESSOR McMOO, PAT AND BO

(and now the fun REALLY starts...)

(about time!)

1903 AD
FIRST TEABAGS INVENTED

THE WILD WEST
MOO-NSTER

Chapter One

A WILD MISSION

It was another sleepy, sunny day on Farmer Barmer's organic farm. Pat Vine, a young bullock, was sitting in a field with his sister, Little Bo.

Most farmyard animals would be content to chew the grass and laze in the sunshine.

But Pat and Bo were not most farmyard animals.

"Strike!" Pat cried, knocking over ten twigs with a single old tennis ball. "Hey, Bo! I beat myself at ten-pin bowling again!"

"Why not let me beat you with my hooves?" Bo suggested, chomping on bubble gum while she painted her udder bright red. "I can always use some punching practice!"

Pat rolled his eyes. His sister only cared about fashion and fighting — but Pat preferred puzzles and working things out. They both belonged to a rare breed of cow called the Emmsy-Squares who were just as smart as humans.

"Hey, you two!" came a friendly voice close by. Pat turned to find a large bull with a red-and-white coat jumping over the fence with a screwdriver in one hoof and a small gadget in another. A pair of glasses was perched on his inquisitive nose, and he gave them both a massive grin.

It was Professor Angus McMoo, the cleverest Emmsy-

Square of all – inventor, genius, and tea-drinking hero extraordinaire!

Pat beamed back. "Hello, Professor. What are you up to?"

"Say 'cheese'," said McMoo.

"Cheese," said Pat instantly.

"Why?" grumped Bo, blowing a gum-bubble.

"Because I've just invented a micro-camera that prints full-sized pictures and I want to test it!" McMoo held up his small, silver gadget. "So, come on – say 'cheese'!"

Suddenly, a terrible noise howled through the air, like a giant rhino with a loudspeaker stuck in its throat: "YEEEEEEEE-HAAAAAAAAARRRR!"

McMoo frowned and lowered his camera. "That sounded nothing like 'cheese'!"

Little Bo leaped into the air, splattering Pat with red paint as she did so. "What *was* that?"

"Uh-oh." Pat turned up his nose as a large, saggy figure appeared over the hillside. "It's . . . Bessie Barmer!"

McMoo lowered his camera. "I'm certainly not taking her picture – it might crack the lens!"

Bessie was the farmer's wife, and she was horrid. She hated all the animals and couldn't wait to send them off to the butcher's. But today her foul face was twisted into a gruesome gap-toothed grin, and the earth shook as she performed a strange dance.

"What's wrong with her?" wondered McMoo.

Bo frowned. "Where do you want me to start?"

"Woo-hooooo!" Bessie screeched, lumbering towards the cows in her muddy clothes. "Look here, you horrible beefy beggars!" She shook her fat fist, and Pat saw she was clutching something shiny. "I'm RICH! One minute I'm digging a ditch with my bare hands, the next . . . I've struck GOLD!"

"Gold!" Pat gasped (although to human ears it came out as "MOOO", as all cow conversations did).

"Pants!" said Bo, scowling. "Why should that sour-faced old trout have any luck?"

Bessie gave them a nasty smile. "Now I can send all you animals to the butcher and turn this farm into a gold mine instead! I'm RIIIIICH!" And with another "Yee-haaah!" she charged off again.

Pat gulped. "Do you think she means it about the farm, Professor?"

But then a high-pitched bleeping noise came from McMoo's rickety shed in the next field. "Never mind Barmy Barmer!" he cried, turning and charging towards the cow shed. "That signal – it's the C.I.A.!"

Bo whooped with excitement and raced after him, and Pat did his best to keep up. Up until recently, Bessie Barmer had been their only real problem. But since they had been asked to join a crack squad of cattle commandoes from the future, the C.I.A. – short for Cows in Action – life had become a lot more dangerous. And it had all started on the same day that Professor McMoo revealed to Pat and Bo his greatest, most astoundingly secret invention . . .

The day he turned his cow shed into a time machine!

"Is that signal being sent across time, Professor?" Pat called as they neared the noisy shed.

"All the way from the twenty-sixth century, on special cow frequencies," puffed McMoo. "It means the C.I.A. are on yoghurt alert."

"Yoghurt alert?" Bo spluttered. "What's that?"

"It's like a red alert," McMoo explained, barging through the shed doors. "Only creamier and better for you."

"There must be trouble with the F.B.I. again," said Pat grimly as he followed them both inside and closed the doors. F.B.I. stood for the Fed-up Bull Institute – the C.I.A.'s sworn enemies. These furious future bulls had their own time machines, and were always trying to change history in their crazy attempts to take over the world.

The professor pulled his big, bronze

lever that transformed the dingy shed into a staggering time craft. With a rattling, clanking sound, the wooden walls slid away to reveal gleaming instrument panels, busy with buttons and smothered in switches. Leads and cables dropped down from the roof in the flick of a tail, and a huge bank of controls in the shape of a horseshoe slid up from the ground. Towards the back of the shed, a large wardrobe and fitting room rose up from a shallow ditch, stuffed full of clothes from the Stone Age to the Space Age and all times in between.

But right now, Pat's attention was fixed on the large computer screen swinging down from the rafters. It showed a tough-looking black bull with sleek, shiny horns and shades. Beside him stood a large old cow with an oversized udder, smiling kindly down at them.

"It's Yak, Director of the C.I.A.," Pat realized.

"And his boss, Madame Milkbelly the Third," said McMoo, quickly bowing. In the year 2550, this grand old cow ruled kindly over all cattle.

"All right, Yak 'n' Milky?" Bo grinned up at the screen. "What's going down?"

"A nice cup of tea would go down very well," said McMoo with a meaningful look. But Bo only folded her arms and blew another gum-bubble, so Pat hurried off instead to put the kettle on.

"Greetings, my friends," said Madame Milkbelly in her prim voice. "Are you well?"

"We're a bit worried," Pat admitted. "Do you know if this farm is ever turned into a gold mine?"

Yak frowned. "We will look into it," he said. "But we've got real problems here, team. According to a top-secret report, the F.B.I. has been sending ter-moo-nators into the past, to the Old Wild West of America . . ."

Despite the warmth of the teapot, Pat felt a shiver go through him at the thought of ter-moo-nators. They were the F.B.I.'s nastiest agents – half robot, half bull and completely without mercy.

"Their time trail seems to lead to 1875," Madame Milkbelly added.

"Fantastic!" boomed McMoo. "That was the time of cowboy legends like Wyatt Earp and Jesse James, Calamity Jane and Buffalo Bill!"

"Cowboys, huh?" Bo squirted some milk into the bucket of tea Pat was preparing. "Can we hang out with them, Professor?"

"I hope so!" McMoo beamed. "Real cowboys, imagine that!"

Pat noticed Yak's face darkening. McMoo loved history – that was why he had built the time shed in the first place, out of bits he found in a scientist's bins. And so sometimes he acted more like a time tourist than a C.I.A. agent!

Pat passed McMoo the bucket of tea. "Er, maybe Yak doesn't want us to hang out with cowboys . . . ?"

"Too right," said Yak. "We don't know what the F.B.I. is up to in the Wild West, but our spies say it's a real monster of a plan . . ."

"What is more," said Madame Milkbelly, "my great-great-great-great-great-great-plus-one-hundred-and-fifty-more-greats-great-grandmother lived in the Wild West in 1875 . . ."

McMoo almost choked on his tea in alarm. "But if ter-moo-nators go back and squish her . . . that means you would never be born!"

Madame Milkbelly nodded gravely. "Which means I would never have started the C.I.A."

"And if you never started the C.I.A., none of us would be here right now!" Pat's brain boggled. "Holy haystacks, talk about changing the future!"

"I'm fed up with talk," Bo complained. "I want action!"

"And you're going to get it," said McMoo. Draining the tea from his bucket, he starting flicking switches and yanking levers. "We must get back to the Wild West at once and stop the F.B.I. before history is messed up for ever. There's not a second to lose!"

Chapter Two

RUSTLERS OF THE RANGE

In a blaze of purple light, the Time Shed burst into the Wild West of 1875. Pat and Bo pushed open the doors and gasped at the wide-open plain before them. It was brown and dusty. The sun was low in the sky over the red, rocky outcrops that edged the horizon. Here and there, prickly cacti stood to attention like green guards.

"I've never seen so much space in my life!" said Pat, staring round in wonder. "Professor, did cows really live here?"

"Oh yes," McMoo called back, rummaging through the Time Shed's costume cupboard. "Computer – give us the Wild West file."

Writing appeared on the big screen
hanging down from the rafters:

++WILD WEST. ++WIDE OPEN AREA IN WESTERN
NORTH AMERICA BETWEEN 1860 AND 1900, NOT YET
TAKEN OVER BY THE SPREADING POPULATION.
++HUNTERS, COWBOYS, SOLDIERS AND RAILWAY
WORKERS WERE THE FIRST TO SETTLE DOWN AND
CLAIM THESE UNTAMED LANDS. ++PLUS LOTS AND
LOTS OF COWS! ++BECAUSE THERE WASN'T MUCH
GRASS ABOUT, THE CATTLE WERE FREE TO ROAM THE
RANGE FOR MILES AROUND. ++THEN EACH YEAR THEY
WERE ROUNDED UP BY THE COWBOYS WHO WORKED
FOR THE LOCAL RANCH AND HERDED TO MARKET.

"I would tell the cowboys to push off,"
Bo declared, trotting outside and
breathing in the fresh, clean air. "What
a view. It's awesome!"

Pat nodded as he followed her. After
their little fields on the farm, the sheer
size of the range was mind-blowing.

"Lucky old Madame Milkbelly's great-great-great-great-great-great-great-plus-one-hundred-and-fifty-more-greats-great-grandmother living somewhere as brilliant as this!" he declared.

But the next moment, a lasso landed around his neck!

Pat gasped as the rope was pulled tight and he fell to his knees. "Erk!" he gasped.

Bo turned to find two nasty-looking men on horseback had appeared over a

low rocky hillside. They wore cowboy hats, and had red hankies tied around their necks. One was gripping the rope that held Pat. The other, who was wearing dark clothes and had a black patchy beard, was tossing his own lasso at Bo.

Quickly, she dodged aside and grabbed hold of the rope. Then she tugged on it, hard – yanking the bearded man off his horse. He landed with a thud in the dust.

"Nice one, Bo!" gasped Pat.

But Bo wasn't finished with the man yet. She grabbed the rope and started to swing him around and around . . . Then she let go! He went flying into the other man, who tumbled from his horse and landed on a spiky cactus. "Yeoooww!" he yelled, letting go of the rope. In a moment, Pat had pulled himself free.

"What's going on here?" demanded Professor McMoo, storming out of the Time Shed. Pat turned to find the professor dressed in a checked shirt with a waistcoat and tasselled trousers. He wore a ten-gallon hat on his head and a silver ring through his nose – a special C.I.A. invention called a

ringblender. Ringblenders projected a special image that made cows look like people, and translated all languages too. "Well? What are you two up to, trying to steal my prize cows?"

The bearded man looked up at him shiftily, completely convinced that McMoo was as human as he was. "Yeah, well," he drawled. "We thought these two were a couple of strays, didn't we, Jim Bob?"

"Sure did, Henry," said Jim Bob quickly, pulling prickles from his bottom. "Didn't know you had them specially trained as attack cows!"

"Don't play innocent with me," said McMoo. "You're cattle rustlers, aren't you?"

"What are cattle rustlers?" wondered Pat.

"People who steal cattle from ranch-owners," said McMoo quietly.

Jim Bob turned to McMoo. "Listen,

mister, you'd be better off letting us take them than leaving them out here on their own." Jim Bob lowered his voice. "They're in danger . . . from the monster!"

"Monster?" McMoo frowned. "What monster?"

"Why, the Longhorn Monster, of course!" cried Henry. "Dang thing's eating every cow around."

"It's doing us out of business!" Jim Bob complained. "Buffalo, bison, bulls and steers — it ain't choosy, it chews them all up! It has driven whole ranches out of business. Most folk have had to sell their land and move away."

"What does it look like, this monster?" McMoo asked.

"Not many have seen it real close," said Henry gravely. "It whips up a storm every time it shows. But it's gotta be big — it swallows down whole herds of cattle and don't leave nothing behind."

22

"Then it should be easy to track," said McMoo thoughtfully.

"That's true," said Pat. "Imagine the size of its poos!"

"Imagine the smell of them," said Bo with a shiver.

"Yak said that the F.B.I. had a monster of a plan," McMoo reminded them. "But maybe it's a plan *about* a monster. We must find this beast!"

"Mister, anyone would think you was speaking to them cows!" Jim Bob looked puzzled. "What you talking 'bout, anyway? If you're thinking of going after that thing, you may as well give us your cattle right now — 'cos you'll never be seen again!"

Bo scowled. "They're just trying to scare us."

But Pat was staring past her at the nearby dusty slope, and starting to shake. "They're succeeding," he murmured. "Look!"

A strange, green glow was growing brighter at the top of the dusty slope. Then, with a terrifying, ear-splitting roar, a horrifying figure nudged into view. Its two horns were like giant, quivering prongs on top of a head the size of a shed. Glowing white eyes shone like headlamps. A wide, pig-like snout was dribbling green gunge into its massive mouth, where giant fangs nestled like stalactites and stalagmites.

"It's the Longhorn Monster!" screamed Jim Bob. "It's come to get us."

Henry wailed at the top of his lungs. "We're doomed!"

The cows stared in horror as the menacing monster drew closer . . .

Chapter Three

JUST PLAINS CRAZY

"I'm getting out of here!" cried Jim Bob. He jumped on his horse backwards in fright, and clung on as it galloped away.

"Wimp!" Bo yelled after him.

Henry's horse bolted too. Desperately, the rustler lassoed it – and it yanked him away! Soon he was yelling and raising a thick trail of dust as the horse dragged him off into the distance.

"Maybe running's not such a bad idea," said Pat nervously as the bizarre beast rumbled towards them.

"If that thing's been eating cows, I'm going to give it indigestion!" Bo declared – and charged off towards the Longhorn Monster!

"Come back, Bo!" cried McMoo as he and Pat quickly ran after her. "Whatever that thing is, it needs careful study!"

"You can study it once I've clobbered it," Bo offered. But just as she was nearing the mysterious monster, a sudden gale blew up dirt into her face. Coughing and spluttering, half-blinded, Bo struggled onwards, but the wind was getting worse, blowing up into a real dust storm. With sudden panic, she realized it was lifting her off the ground!

Luckily, Pat and the professor grabbed a leg

27

each and pulled her back down the slope – flying her like a cow-shaped kite! At last, the wind died down and she collapsed on the ground in a heap.

"Why did you stop me?" she grumbled. "I was that close to nailing the monster."

"Afraid not, Bo." McMoo pointed into the distance, where a little cloud of dirt was being chased by a far larger one. "Seems the monster was distracted by Henry the rustler making tracks across the plain."

"Of course!" Pat nodded. "It must have thought Henry's dust trail belonged to some stampeding cattle, and decided to chase after him."

"It's going too fast for us to catch it up now," said Bo crossly. "Pants!"

"Speaking of pants, you should put some on," said McMoo, pulling two ringblenders from his pocket. "It's time you got into human disguise, like me."

Pat nodded. "Between rustlers and monsters, cows seem to be top targets around here. The sooner we look like humans the better!"

Reluctantly, Bo followed Pat into the Time Shed and got changed into a wig and a long, flowing green silk dress with lots of frills and flounces. Pat put on a pair of brown trousers and a blue checked shirt, and wore a cowboy hat over his horns.

Then he and Bo took a look in the Time Shed's special mirror, which showed them how they would appear to humans.

"Check me out," said Pat, who looked like a fresh-faced young farmhand. "From boy cow to cowboy!"

"This look is lame," complained Bo, unimpressed with her piled-up wig of red hair. "Can't I rip this dress a bit, spray-paint it pink and wear it with a crocodile-skin rucksack?"

"No," said McMoo flatly. "We want to fit in around here, not stand out like . . . ah."

"Like 'ah'?" Bo frowned. "What does that mean?"

"It means we've got company!" her brother hissed.

Like McMoo, Pat had just noticed a wiry old man standing in the doorway, caked in dust. It covered every bit of him from his cracked leather boots to his wild beard and hair.

"Where am I?" the old man wondered. He tried to wipe his small round glasses on his shirt sleeve but only made them muckier. "What is this place?"

Not wanting to give away their big secret, Pat quickly tugged on the lever that turned the Time Shed into an ordinary barn again. With a rattling, clanking noise, the controls vanished back into the walls and floor.

The old man stared about short-sightedly. "What in tarnation was that?"

"Er, just some creaky floorboards," said Pat quickly.

"This is my farmhouse," said the professor. "My name's McMoo, and these are my farmhands, Pat and Bo."

"Well, my name's Old Josh Hosh," the old man told them. "I was just on my way into town when a dang dust storm half-buried me and scared away my horse . . ."

Pat looked at McMoo. "Sounds like they had a run-in with the Longhorn Monster too."

"Don't mention that Longhorn Monster!" cried Josh Hosh. "I hate that pesky creature!" He stamped his foot on the floor, then coughed in the cloud of dust he created.

"Come here, old-timer," said Bo. With unexpected gentleness she dusted him down, licked his glasses clean with her slobbery tongue and spat out the dust on the floor.

"Why, thank you, missy!" said Josh, squinting at her through his sticky

glasses. "You folks been living out here long?"

McMoo cleared his throat. "Er, not very."

"Well, you've built a house out here," said Josh. "And the law says that if you live here for a few years this land will become yours to keep, free of charge."

"Ah yes!" The professor smiled. "The Homestead Act, passed in 1862!"

Pat looked at the mini-mountains of dust at Josh's feet. "I think he's brought most of the land in with him!"

"Wish I'd built a nice, cheap and easy barn like this," Josh went on, sighing. "But I'm a miner, and I found me some silver a few miles from here. I spent every cent I had hiring workers to dig out tunnels and shafts, ready to mine me a fortune. But then" – he bunched up his wrinkled fists – "that monster showed up and attacked my men! It scared 'em all away, so bad that they ain't never coming back!"

"Is that why you're going into town, Josh?" asked Pat. "To find some more workers?"

"Nope. No one will come out here, except for crazy folks like you." Josh stood up. "So I'm selling my mine, then I'm getting out of this dang county." He sniffed. "Driven away by the Longhorn Monster, just like everyone else."

McMoo nodded. "Well, if you don't mind, Old Josh, I think we'll tag along with you."

Pat blinked. "We will?"

"You think I'd pass on the chance to see a real Wild West town?" The professor's eyes were sparkling. "Besides, you heard Josh – there's no one out here on the plains. If we want to find out more, the nearest town is our best bet. So, let's jump to it . . ." He straightened his hat and smiled. "Cowboy style!"

Chapter Four

DANGER IN DODGEM

The town of Dodgem was a two-hour trek away. By the time McMoo and his friends reached its backstreets, night had well and truly fallen.

Pat shook his aching hoofs. "I'm glad the monster left us alone."

"Alone is the right word," said Bo, looking about the dark, dusty street. Tall, shadowy wooden buildings loomed either side of them like giant gravestones. Hitching posts stood here and there for tying up horses, all of them empty. "Where is everybody?"

Old Josh sighed. "Like I told you, missy — most folks have moved away to somewhere monster-free."

"So how are you going to sell your mine?" McMoo wondered.

"I have heard there's one person in town who's rich enough and greedy enough to take it off my hands," said Old Josh. "She lives above the Last-Chance-But-One Saloon on Main Street, and her name is Beepy Bee."

"Beepy Bee?" Bo snorted. "She sounds dumb!"

"They say she's very mean," said Old Josh nervously. "Even so, I ain't got no choice but to deal with her."

They walked on through the deserted town until they reached Main Street. Here there were shops and stores and saloon bars – some of which actually had lights on – and the sound of piano playing and raised voices floated through the night air.

"At last," said Pat, "signs of life!" Even as he spoke, a cowboy came flying out through the swinging doors

of a nearby saloon and landed with a thud at his feet.

Bo frowned. "Maybe 'life' is too strong a word!"

Pat and McMoo helped up the cowboy, who quickly staggered away into the bar opposite. Moments later, a dark-haired man with a cowboy gun came out and walked up to Professor McMoo. A silver star was pinned to his leather waistcoat.

"It's the sheriff!" Josh whispered. "The local lawman."

"So . . ." The sheriff eyed McMoo gravely. "Stranger, huh?"

"Not as strange as some!" McMoo smiled. "We're headed for the Last-Chance-But-One Saloon."

The sheriff scowled. "You carrying weapons?"

"No way!" cried Pat.

"Better take this, then," said the sheriff, passing Pat a cowboy gun. "It gets kind of rough in there!" Even as he spoke, two more cowboys came smashing through a window further down the street. "That's the saloon you're looking for," said the Sheriff, walking away. "Good luck."

Suddenly, McMoo noticed that the only other places still open were a glass-repair store and an undertaker's!

"Er, couldn't you come in with us?" asked McMoo.

"You gotta be kidding!" The sheriff burst into hysterical laughter as he walked off. "I ain't crazy!"

"He's scared of going in there," Bo realized, rubbing her hooves together with glee. "This is going to be fun!"

"We're going inside a real Wild West saloon!" McMoo agreed. "Imagine that!"

"I'm not sure I want to," Pat admitted as Old Josh led the way inside.

The saloon was a large, hot room that smelled of sweat and gunsmoke. At the back of the room was a flight of tatty stairs leading to a broken balcony. Fans turned feebly in the high ceiling, trying to cool the crowds of men in cowboy hats. Some were talking at tables, some lay flat out on the dirty wooden floor. Everyone looked unhappy. Some of the men were even crying.

"I've lost all my cows," said one cowboy sadly.

"Me too," added another, blowing his nose. He picked up a banjo, cleared his

40

throat and started to sing a slow, sad
cowboy song:

"I miss you, my cow!
I miss you, and how!
I shiver, I shake and I shudder.
I miss your cow trail,
Your hooves and your tail,
Your two eyes, your nose and your udder!"

"How wet!" Bo complained loudly.

"Shh!" said Pat. "He'll start crying
again!"

Josh went up to the barkeeper, a tall,
skinny man who served all the drinks.
"Good evening," he said. "I'm here to
see Beepy Bee."

Suddenly, the whole saloon fell silent
and everyone stared at him.

The barkeeper narrowed his eyes.
"You sure you want to see Beepy Bee?"

"Er . . . yes," said Josh. "I want to sell
her my silver mine."

"Beepy Bee don't buy nothing,"
croaked an old man on the floor with a

beard the size of a badger. "She *wins* stuff. I tried to sell her my gold mine. But she made me gamble it away on a game of cards."

"What game?" asked McMoo.

"Snap!" said another sorry-looking man sitting in a nasty puddle on the floor. "She's the best Snap player in the world! She beat me hands down and won my copper mine."

"She won my whole ranch," wailed another miserable cowboy.

"And every scrap of land I owned," sobbed another. "She never loses."

Pat frowned. "But why does she want to win the local people's land and mines and stuff?" he wondered. "Isn't she scared of the Longhorn Monster?"

"She ain't scared of nothing and nobody," the barkeeper declared, pointing to a flight of stairs at the back of the saloon. "And here she comes now!"

The saloon fell even more silent. McMoo, Pat and Bo looked over – and gasped.

A large woman in tassled leather trousers and a bulging waistcoat was lumbering down the stairs. A cowboy hat was jammed on top of her head, and her fat face was fixed in a fierce scowl.

"That's Beepy Bee?" Pat blinked. "But . . . she looks just like Bessie Barmer from the farm!"

Bo groaned. "It must be another of her rubbishy relatives. We meet them wherever we end up!"

"Never mind Bessie's ancestor," hissed McMoo. "Look who's coming down the stairs after her!"

To anyone else in the saloon, the two towering figures behind Beepy looked like mean cowboys you wouldn't want to mess with. But the C.I.A. agents could see through the newcomers' disguises – and quickly ducked out of sight behind the bar. Because the two figures clanking down the stairs had glowing green eyes, mechanical hooves and gleaming metal horns . . .

They were both ter-moo-nators!

Chapter Five

A BRAWL ON THE CARDS

"Well, well," muttered McMoo, peeping up from behind the bar. "Looks like yet another Barmer is working for the F.B.I."

The large woman glared around the silent saloon. "The name's Barmer. Big-Pants Barmer."

Pat frowned. "I thought her name was Beepy."

"Josh thought her name was Beepy Bee," McMoo whispered. "But that's just the sound of her initials spelled out B–P–B!"

Trembling, Old Josh stepped forward. "I wanna sell you my silver mine, Miss Barmer."

"Don't call me Miss!" shouted Big-Pants. She pulled out a gun and shot his hat off. "I *never* miss!"

"S-s-s-sorry, Big-Pants," said Josh, snatching up his fallen hat. "But please, won't you buy my mine? It's out on the west range and it's worth at least twenty thousand dollars . . ."

"It ain't worth nothing," snarled Big-Pants. "Not with that mangy monster on the loose out there." She put her gun away and smiled, showing a mouth full of broken teeth. "But I'm a kind, sweet person really. I'll play a game with you. Beat me at Snap, and I'll give you twenty thousand dollars – you can even keep your stupid mine. But if I beat you, I get it for free and you get nothing!"

Old Josh gulped. "OK," he said, shaking Big-Pants' hand. "Guess I ain't got much choice."

Behind the bar, Bo hissed in McMoo's ear: "Professor, we can't let Josh go through with this. You heard what everyone said – Big-Pants never loses!"

"I wonder why that is," said McMoo thoughtfully. "Bo, you and I had better keep an eye on her."

"What can I do, Professor?" asked Pat eagerly.

McMoo passed Pat his special micro-camera. "Sneak upstairs to Big-Pants Barmer's room and look for clues. We must find out what the F.B.I. is up to."

"A proper spy mission!" Pat gulped. "I shan't let you down, Professor."

McMoo grinned. "I know."

"Take care, little bruv," said Bo.

His heart pounding, Pat crept away through the crowd of cowboys. Big-Pants

Barmer and her bullish bodyguards were pushing people out of the way, clearing a path to a table in the corner. While everyone was watching them, Pat ran up the stairs and vanished from view.

Big-Pants sat down on two chairs at once while Old Josh perched on a stool opposite. A crowd quickly gathered around them, allowing McMoo and Bo to sneak nearer on all fours.

The professor peeped through a cowboy's legs and saw one of the ter-moo-nators offer Old Josh a pack of Snap cards. Old Josh shuffled them and handed them back. The ter-moo-nator smiled. He dealt half the cards to Josh and half to Big-Pants.

"The first one to get three Snaps wins the game," Big-Pants growled.

As she spoke, McMoo noticed the other ter-moo-nator press a button on a small square gadget fixed beneath the table. "I wonder what that does," he murmured.

Old Josh turned over his first card with a trembling hand. The card showed a shaggy buffalo wearing a crown.

Big-Pants started to turn over her own card — "SNAP!" she yelled.

Sure enough, the gargantuan gunslinger had turned over the exact same card on her first go!

"That was lucky," Bo remarked.

"But not for Josh," said McMoo.

Old Josh gulped and turned over another card. It showed a cow holding a big gun.

"SNAP!" Big-Pants yelled – before she had even picked up her card! The crowd gasped in disbelief. But sure enough, as she laid the card down on the table, everyone saw it was another perfect match.

"I don't believe it!" cried Josh. "You must be cheating!"

"How could I be cheating?" Big-Pants grinned nastily. "You shuffled them cards yourself, old-timer, remember? Now, get playing!"

McMoo chewed his hoof nervously. "If Big-Pants beats him again, she'll get his mine – and Josh will get nothing!"

The onlookers held their breaths as Old Josh slapped down another card – a picture of a fly buzzing round a cowpat. Big-Pants smiled and reached to turn over her own card . . .

But suddenly the saloon bar doors crashed open and a large, angry-looking man barged in. "I've come for you, Big-Pants!" he yelled.

Bo stared in surprise. The man's hat was as big and red as his droopy moustache. His clothes were dark and dirty, and his fists were hairy and huge.

"Well, well," sneered Big-Pants. "If it ain't Lobster Lobo, owner of the largest gold mine in the state – until I won it in a game of Snap and left *you* in a state!"

"You cheated me," Lobster snarled. "And I've come back to teach you a lesson!"

"You couldn't teach a cactus to grow spikes!" Big-Pants replied.

Lobster strode forward, raising his fists. But before he was halfway across the saloon, one of the ter-moo-nators charged towards him. The next moment – WHAM! – Lobster was butted backwards and crashed heavily into three burly men.

"Hey, get off!" the men shouted – and shoved Lobster away into a couple of cowboys. In return, the furious cowboys attacked the men . . .

And suddenly a huge bar fight broke out!

McMoo ducked down as the fists started flying. Wrestling cowboys staggered this way and that, all across the saloon. Bottles were broken. Chairs were hurled through the air. Tables were smashed in two.

"Cool, Professor!" Bo whooped and whacked one big bruiser in the chops while tripping another. "I was beginning to think the west wasn't really wild after all!"

But Big-Pants seemed less than pleased. "Quit brawlin', you knuckleheads!" she shouted, flattening anyone who came near. "I was just about to win the old-timer's mine, fair and square!"

Old Josh gasped as a cowboy fell into his lap – and suddenly he was caught up in the fighting too! Bo quickly picked the old man up and carried him clear.

"That girl must be as strong as a carthorse," the barkeeper declared.

"A horse?" Bo squirted milk in his eye. "How cheeky!"

"Don't draw attention to yourself, Bo!" McMoo hissed. "Remember, the ter-moo-nators can see through our ringblender disguises, just as we can see through theirs— OOF!" The next moment, a flying beer mug whacked him between the horns and sent him sprawling beneath the card table.

"Professor!" Bo shouted in alarm, picking her way through the furious fighting, trying to get to him. "Hang on, I'm coming!"

But then suddenly a dark figure loomed up in front of her, its green eyes aglow — one of the ter-moo-nators!

"Warning!" Its mechanical voice grated in her ears. "Female C.I.A. agent detected."

"You'd better believe it," said Bo crossly, standing her ground as the fight raged on around them. "Now, get out of my way!"

"You will get out of *our* way," came another grating voice. "C.I.A. scum!"

Bo whirled round to find the other ter-moo-nator was right behind her. Both robo-bulls reached out for her with metal hooves ...

She was trapped!

Chapter Six

PANTS ON FIRE!

Bo ducked down as the ter-moo-nators lunged for her — and the robo-bulls wound up clonking each other! Quickly she shoved past them, trying to reach Big-Pants' card table and the professor. But as she fought her way through the quarrelling crowd, she suddenly saw that Big-Pants Barmer was pointing a cowboy gun straight at her!

"Hold it, girlie," Big-Pants shouted. "Or you'll have more holes than a cactus got prickles!"

Bo knew she had no choice. Angrily, she raised her hooves in the air. She could hear the clanking of ter-moo-nators coming up behind her, closed her eyes, braced herself . . .

But suddenly she found herself hauled out of the way – by Lobster Lobo!

He turned and dragged Bo after him through the fighting crowd. "Come on, girlie – any enemy of Big-Pants is a pal of mine."

Bo grinned. "Cheers, Crab!"

He frowned. "The name's Lobster!"

"Whatever," said Bo, staggering out through the saloon doors. "But we've got to get my friend the professor out too. He could be hurt!"

Even as she spoke, the one remaining window in the saloon was smashed to pieces as one of the angry ter-moo-nators charged through it.

"There is no escape," grated the ter-moo-nator, pulling a ray gun from a holster around his metal hips. "Now you will be TER-MOO-NATED!"

Upstairs in Big-Pants Barmer's bedroom, Pat heard all the commotion and hoped Bo and the professor were all right.

In the bottom of a drawer, beneath a pile of especially big pants, he found a thick file full of important-looking papers with lots of legal words he didn't understand.

Pat laid the papers out on the half-broken bed and took lots of pictures with the professor's special micro-camera. Each time he pressed the button, a small square of paper popped out of a tiny slot in the back, ready to be unfolded into a proper photograph.

Then he heard a familiar yell from

outside: "Keep back, techno-beef, or I'll kick you in the printed circuits!"

"Bo!" Pat gasped, and rushed to the window. There she stood in the street below, beside a large man with an even larger moustache. They were both facing up to an armed ter-moo-nator!

Thinking fast, Pat grabbed the enormous pants from the drawer and hurled himself out of the window! "Geronimoooo!" he yelled as he was swept through the air, landing with a clang on the ter-moo-nator's back.

The robo-bull toppled over and
squashed its own gun – and before it
could recover, Pat pulled the pants down
over its head!

"Thanks for dropping in, Pat!" cried
Bo. As the ter-moo-nator pulled in a
panic at the billowing material, Bo
landed her hardest double-hoof
haymaker right on its horns. With a
sizzling sound, sparks jumped from the
ter-moo-nator's head – and the pants
started to smoke! The metal monster ran

off down the street, mooing loudly, until
it stumbled into a dirty water trough
and lay there, quietly steaming.

"We rock!" cried Bo, grabbing Pat in
a hug. "Sure you didn't hurt yourself
when you landed?"

Pat smiled and shook his head.
"Luckily those pants caught the wind as
I fell."

"I hate to think what wind they
usually catch," said the big man with
the bigger moustache. "Thanks for your

help, kid. Lobster Lobo, at your service."

Pat shook his hand and looked around. "But where's the professor?"

"Here!" cried McMoo, striding out through the saloon doors. He glanced over at the smoking ter-moo-nator with the pants on its head, and a smile spread over his face. "Looks like someone is quick on the *drawers* round here!"

"It was Pat!" said Bo proudly.

"Did you find anything in Big-Pants' room?" McMoo asked. "Aside from big pants, I mean."

Pat nodded excitedly, and was about to reach for his photos when he realized the saloon had fallen quiet. "Hey, what happened to the fighting?"

"It's over." McMoo wiped his mouth. "I persuaded the barkeeper to give everyone free cups of tea – a hot milky brew takes the fight out of you!"

"But are you OK, Professor?" asked Bo. "I saw you fall under the table."

"Correct," McMoo agreed. "And I stayed lying down so I could study an F.B.I. gadget hidden there – a special card-changing device!"

Pat frowned. "A what?"

"It automatically changes Big-Pants' card to match whichever card is lying on the table," McMoo explained. "So she gets Snap every time."

"Why that no-good, low-down, yellow-bellied, black-hearted, purple-kneed, green-toed rattlesnake!" cried Lobster Lobo. "I knew she cheated me. Let's get her!"

McMoo held up his hoof. "Please don't disturb her, Mr Lobo. She and Old Josh have started playing cards again – and in all the confusion, I cleverly reversed the card-changer's settings so it will work for Old Josh instead!"

"Yeeeeee-hahhh!" Old Josh's cry echoed out of the saloon. "I've beaten ole Baggy-Pants!" The next moment he came tearing outside with a hat full of dollar bills. "I've got her twenty thousand dollars and I've still got my mine! Wa-heyyy!" He started running around hugging anything in sight: Bo, Pat, Lobster, a hitching post and – unfortunately – a cactus. "OW!"

"Laugh it up while you can, old-timer!" snarled Big-Pants, striding out of the saloon with the other ter-moo-nator close behind her. "I want my cash back, Josh Hosh — or else you and your friends here are in deep trouble."

"You don't scare us," shouted Lobster. "I'm buddies with three of the most famous gunslingers in the west — Jesse James, Buffalo Bill and Calamity Jane. They're gonna come here and sort you out, just wait!"

"But they ain't around to help none of you now," Big-Pants gloated, waggling her cowboy gun at him. "Are they?"

"Maybe they ain't — but I am," came a voice Pat recognized. It belonged to the sheriff! He was standing behind them looking very grumpy, with a cowboy gun in each hand. "I don't mind you folks trashing a saloon," he went on, "but I won't have any trouble on the streets of Dodgem!"

McMoo smiled at Big-Pants and the ter-moo-nator. "We were just leaving!

Weren't we, everyone?"

"Wait," growled the ter-moo-nator. The scarf around his neck had fallen away, and a plate on his steel chest revealed his name was T-65. "You have been identified as C.I.A. agent Angus McMoo. Danger rating: A-plus."

"Thank you," said McMoo coldly. "But I aim to be A-double-plus by the time this is over!"

"I'm warning you – I've had enough!" the sheriff shouted. "Anyone still out on the street in ten seconds is gonna get a belly full of lead!"

Pat clutched his tummy. "Let's go!"

"You ain't heard the last of this," Big-Pants promised them. "Just watch out for the Longhorn Monster — at night they say it gets very, very HUNGRY."

"Ignore her," said McMoo, tipping his hat at the sheriff as he led his gang away down the deserted street. But he couldn't help a shiver as the mocking laughter of Big-Pants and the ter-moo-nator echoed after them.

Chapter Seven

WIND OF THE MONSTER

McMoo and the others walked the dark and dusty backstreets of Dodgem. The professor's nose was buried in the photos Pat had taken of Big-Pants' papers, and Pat had to keep nudging him this way and that to stop him walking into a wall or a cactus.

"Do those pictures actually tell you anything?" Bo questioned.

"They tell me Big-Pants is buying up miles and miles of land in the Wild West," McMoo announced. "And she must be buying it for the F.B.I."

"But how can she afford it?" asked Pat.

"By cheating the likes of Lobster out

of their mines," the professor explained. "The F.B.I. must mine out the gold and silver and use it to buy *more* land . . ."

Pat nodded. "And everyone's selling up cheap because of the monster. Do you think it's something horrid they brought back from the future?"

Bo shrugged. "Or the past. Maybe it's a dinosaur?"

"Hey!" said Lobster, shuffling to a stop. "I don't understand a cotton-picking word you're saying, but look – we've run out of streets!"

They had reached the edge of town. Now only the dark, wide-open plains stretched scarily ahead of them.

"The nearest town is twenty miles by stagecoach," said Old Josh. "But the coach won't come a-calling till tomorrow."

Bo turned to Lobster. "Do you think your Wild West gunslinger mates will be on that coach?"

"I dunno." He sighed. "I sent Bill, Jesse and Calamity a letter. But they never replied."

"Well, we can't stay here and wait for a stagecoach in any case," McMoo announced. "Big-Pants and her even-bigger buddy will be out to get us — unless the sheriff gets us first!"

"Let's go back to the Time Shed," Pat suggested. "Er, I mean, our farmhouse."

"Yes, we'll be safe there," McMoo agreed.

"Provided the monster doesn't eat us on the way," said Bo.

Swapping uneasy looks, the others followed her into the cold, inky darkness of the endless plain . . .

The gang made good progress for the first hour. Bo had kicked over various boulders and cacti on their way from the Time Shed to Dodgem, and now she was using them to guide their way back.

"Wait a minute," said Pat nervously.
An eerie green glow was lighting up the
nearest hillside. "What's that?"

Then his stomach did a back flip and
a triple somersault as a horrible howl
ripped through the night.

"Oh no!" groaned McMoo. "Not
again!"

"It's the Longhorn Monster!" cried
Old Josh.

73

Lobster yelped. "It's going to get us!"
The luminous monster loomed up over
the brow of the rocky hillside, as big as
a radioactive bus. With its huge horns
quivering, massive mouth drooling and
enormous nose running it made a truly
terrifying sight. As its massive,
unblinking eyes fixed upon him, Pat
pulled out the micro-camera and tried
to take pictures – but the same stinging
wind as before had blown up, whipping
grit into his eyes.

Pat stumbled and almost fell. But then someone grabbed hold of his arm. "C'mon, kid," growled Lobster Lobo. "We can't stay here."

"No, wait!" Pat shoved the camera back in his pocket with shaking hooves. "Professor, Bo, where are you?"

"Run!" Lobster insisted. The monster roared again and the ground shook as it rumbled towards them. Lobster grabbed Pat by the arm and dragged him away through the driving wind.

Pat choked on dust, and his skin stung all over as he stumbled across the dark and rocky plains. His heart was pounding so hard he thought it might explode. Time lost all meaning as he and Lobster staggered on through the blinding gale — but as he blinked the last of the grit from his eyes, Pat finally saw the green glow of the monster vanishing behind a rocky rise.

"We made it," Lobster declared.

"But what happened to the professor and Bo?" Pat asked fearfully.

"I'm sure they're all right," said Lobster gruffly. "We'll find them back at your farmhouse, you'll see."

"I'm not sure we will," said Pat miserably, staring around at the moonlit plain. "I don't know the way from here!"

Lobster rolled his eyes. "In that case, let's head for my mine."

"But it's not yours any more," Pat reminded him.

"We'll see about that," said Lobster. Clenching his big fists, he set off into the night.

Hoping Bo and the professor were OK, Pat followed him.

Not so very far away, Professor McMoo, Bo and Old Josh were wandering the shadowy plains themselves. They had run and run until the monster lost their scent — but now they had lost their way.

"I do hope Pat is all right." McMoo sighed as the sun rose slowly from behind the mountains.

"He's a tough bullock," Bo assured him. "And he's got Sea Cucumber looking after him."

"Lobster!" McMoo reminded her.

"Whatever." Bo shrugged. "Bet they're waiting for us in the Time Shed already — and now it's daylight, that will be easier to spot."

"Hey!" said Old Josh. "*I've* just spotted my old silver mine!" He pointed to a large cave in a reddish cliffside, not far away. Wooden huts of various sizes were dotted about outside.

"Perhaps we could stop there for a cup of tea," McMoo suggested. "Then we can carry on searching."

He led the way over to the mine. But just as they were nearing the biggest of

the huts – the ground in front of them was blasted with lasers! Old Josh jumped in the air in surprise and landed in Bo's arms.

"Hold it!" came a familiar voice – and Big-Pants Barmer jumped out from behind a nearby rock. Ter-moo-nator T-65 was just behind her.

"Ah," said McMoo. "No tea, then."

"You may have got away from the monster," said the ter-moo-nator as it pulled out its gun, "but you will not get away from these LASER BLASTS . . ."

"Run!" McMoo shouted – and he kicked up a big cloud of dust with his hooves. The ter-moo-nator fired wildly through the blinding haze. Bo felt a sizzling blast whizz past her ear, and another strike the ground at Old Josh's feet. But McMoo lowered his head and bashed open the door to one of the wooden huts. Bo and Josh followed him inside and slammed the door shut.

"Ain't no use hiding here," Old Josh panted. "There's nowhere to go. It's just a storehouse!"

Bullets and laser blasts smashed into the wooden walls. Smouldering cinders showered over them.

"This place wouldn't keep out a determined hamster," McMoo agreed. The gunfire outside grew louder. "Old Josh is right – it looks like we're finished!"

Chapter Eight

A MINER PROBLEM

The sun was rising over the distant,
craggy mountains as Pat and Lobster
neared the gold mine. It seemed
deserted. But as Pat quickened his step
up a rocky hillside, Lobster suddenly
stopped still.

"Look!" he hissed, peering over the
brow of the hill. "Cattle rustlers!"

Pat frowned to see two familiar
men standing guard over some bulls
in the shade of an extra-large cactus.
"Henry and Jim Bob!" he whispered,
remembering his close encounter with
them outside the Time Shed. "They
found a few cows left on the range
after all."

"No time to set them cows free right

now," said Lobster. "We should press on
to my mine. If you help me sling out
whoever's in there, I'll help you find that
farmhouse of yours."

Pat thought longingly of the safety of
the Time Shed. The professor and Bo
were bound to get there just as soon as
they could. "OK, then," he agreed. He
felt sorry for the captured cows, but
maybe he could rescue them later.

They pressed on, keeping out of sight
of the rustlers, until they reached the
entrance to Lobster's mine. Pat noticed
strange markings in the dirt. Some were
clearly hoofprints, while others were
long and wide and deep. "What do you
think made these?"

"Let's look in the mine," murmured
Lobster. He took a lantern hanging
from the wall, lit it with a match, and
led the way down a cold, dark
underground tunnel. In the smoky light,
Pat found some hoofmarks in the dirt,

crusty old cowpats and scraps of leftover hay.

"Someone's been keeping cows here!" Lobster exclaimed.

"Of course – that's why Big-Pants has been after people's mines," Pat realized. "Everyone thinks they've all been eaten by the monster or scared away – when all the time they've been hidden down mines like yours!"

"Why does Big-Pants want to hide cows?" Lobster wondered. "Is she jealous 'cos they're all better looking than her?"

"She's working for people who are very interested in cows," Pat explained. "But where are they now?" He stuck his hands in his pockets and found some squares of paper there – the photographs he had taken with the micro-camera. "I forgot about these. It was so dusty and windy I don't suppose anything came out . . ." But then, as he looked at one photograph, he gasped.

Lobster frowned. "What?"

Pat stared at him. "I know the secret of the Longhorn Monster!"

"Well it'll have to wait!" Lobster hissed, putting a finger to his lips. "Sounds like someone's coming!"

Pat listened hard – and suddenly his blood ran cold.

Sinister scuffles and footsteps were echoing down the tunnel towards them . . .

Across the plain, in Old Josh's storehouse, all Bo could hear was the sizzle of laser blasts and the BANG-BANG of bullets as the walls were chipped away around them.

Old Josh held his ears. "Big-Pants and her buddy could zap this whole shack to pieces with them magic fire bolts," he moaned. "What's keeping 'em?"

"They're playing with us," said Bo angrily.

"Not just that," cried Professor McMoo. "Josh, you've still got Big-Pants' twenty thousand dollars – she must want it in one piece."

Old Josh pulled out his wad of banknotes and kissed it. "Me too!"

"Any ideas, Prof?" asked Bo.

"Yes – duck!" McMoo advised as the storehouse shook and a pile of boxes beside him tumbled to the ground. The lid of one of them cracked open – to reveal several brown tubes, like chunky fireworks.

McMoo gasped. "Bless my horns! Sticks of dynamite — a powerful explosive!"

"I forgot I stored that here," cried Old Josh. "I used dynamite to blast away the rock down below so I could get to the silver."

"Awesome!" Bo cried. But suddenly a smouldering plank fell from the wall and landed on top of the dynamite — and sparks started streaming out from one of the sticks!

"Uh-oh!" said McMoo. "The scorched wood has set light to the fuse! The dynamite's going to explode!"

"I'll put it out!" Bo declared. She squirted milk on the stick of dynamite. Nothing happened. She beat her hooves on the fuse to put out the sparks, but they kept spitting back into life.

Old Josh whacked it with a shovel. McMoo tried sitting on it. In desperation Bo did a tap dance on the

explosive and hammered it into the
ground – but it seemed nothing could
put out the fizzling fuse!

"TAKE COVER!" shouted McMoo.

Old Josh jumped in a barrel, and
McMoo and Bo hid behind a stack of
heavy wooden timbers.

Then, a split-second later – KAAA-
BLAAAAMM!

With a noise like thunder, the
dynamite exploded. Bo gasped as it
blew off the roof and flattened the walls.
A fireball rose up into the sky and the

air filled with a choking black smoke. "Whoaaaaa!" yelled Old Josh as his barrel was blown away by the blast, rolling off at incredible speed . . .

And with a thrill of fear, Bo felt the ground crack and crumble beneath her hooves. "Argh!" she yelled as she and the professor fell through the floor into cold, clammy darkness . . .

"Oof!" gasped McMoo as he landed on his back – and then "oof" again as Bo landed on his stomach! His third "oof" came as burning boxes and blazing wood started tumbling down around them.

Bo quickly hitched up her dress and started putting out the fires with some well-aimed squirts from her udder.

"Leave that bit," McMoo said, picking up a piece of wood burning at one end like a giant candle. "We can use it to light our way."

"What happened?" asked Bo, looking up at daylight through the jagged hole in the roof.

"The dynamite cracked open the ground beneath us," McMoo explained. "We must have dropped down into a mine tunnel running beneath the storeroom."

Bo gulped. "Where's Old Josh?"

"He was hiding inside a tough barrel – he should be OK," said McMoo. "But at the speed he was rolling, he'll be dizzy for a week!"

"Perhaps he'll roll all the way to the Time Shed," said Bo hopefully. "That way, he'll bump into Pat and Jellyfish."

McMoo groaned. "For the last time, you mean LOB—"

"Shhh!" Bo could hear voices floating down through the hole in the tunnel roof. She quickly ducked away out of sight.

"Nothing left!" Big-Pants was wailing. "My beautiful loot! It must have been blown to bits along with them no-good nuisances!"

"We shall soon win more money," T-65 told her. "And now no one can stop us taking this mine. It is a shame I could not question McMoo. But at least if he is ter-moo-nated he can no longer meddle with our plans."

The ter-moo-nator clanked away, and Big-Pants trailed crossly after him.

"Ter-moo-nated?" McMoo smiled. "Not on your nelly!" He bounced up and down in excitement. "Come on, Bo! We've got the chance to explore a

real-life Wild West silver mine —
imagine that! Come on, let's try this
way . . ."

He trotted off down the tunnel with
his flaming torch. But soon McMoo
and Bo had to get down on all fours
to keep going. Then they had to
wriggle forward on their bellies.

"Maybe we should turn back," Bo whispered.

"We can't turn back now," McMoo told her as he turned the next corner. "I can see light at the end of the tunnel!

"Must be the way out!" said Bo excitedly.

McMoo frowned. "Or a way *in* . . ."

The professor reached the end of the tunnel and flopped down onto a ledge below. Now his bottom was out of her face, Bo realized the tunnel came out high up in a massive underground cavern that stretched on as far as the eye could see. She blinked in the bright white light of a massive lamp in the high rocky ceiling. It shone like a mini-sun over hundreds of human-style shacks and ranches, linked by little gardens and dusty roads.

Bo's jaw dropped open so far her bubblegum nearly fell out. "Professor," she breathed, joining him on the ledge.

"What's going on?"

"I don't know, Bo," murmured McMoo, putting down the torch.

They stared down at the village in amazement. Working in every garden, cooking in every kitchen and strolling down every pathway . . . were cows!

Chapter Nine

COW-NTRY FOLK

"This is crazy, Professor!" Bo protested. "Who would build a town underground and give it to cows, bulls and buffalos?"

McMoo studied the smoothness of the rock wall sloping down towards the village. "The whole cavern has been hollowed out using technology from the future," he reported. "This is the F.B.I.'s work."

"But why?" Bo wondered.

"That's what we have to find out," said McMoo grimly.

Suddenly they heard a familiar, echoing, grinding roar. "The Longhorn Monster!" Bo hissed. Sure enough, a giant, monstrous shape came crawling into sight along the main road, growling deeply as it advanced on the village. Its lengthy horns quivered on top of its huge head, and its dusty skin glowed eerily even in the daylight. Then the monster slowed to a stop, wide eyes shining from its gruesome face like headlights . . .

But suddenly the monster's eyes went dark, as if they'd been switched off.

They really *were* headlights!

McMoo gasped. "The monster isn't a monster at all – it's a machine!"

Suddenly, with a loud, creaking, croaking noise, a big flap in the monster's backside swung open and formed a ramp leading down to the road. Bo stared in disbelief as seven or eight buffalos were herded out by a ter-moo-nator.

Bo gasped. "It's a secret cow-carrier!"

"Very ingenious," muttered McMoo. "Disguised as a monster to scare away the humans, so it can pick up cows

without resistance. It can even kick up
its own dust storm to stop anyone
tracking it. The F.B.I. wouldn't want any
witnesses while they drop off their stolen
cattle at mines like this one."

Bo boggled at him. "You think there are other underground villages beneath other mines?"

"You can see how big this place is," said McMoo, sweeping a hoof round at the gigantic cavern. "The mines must make handy exits and entrances all around the area – that's why the F.B.I. are buying them all up!"

The ter-moo-nator on the ramp spoke briefly to a brown bison wearing a construction worker's coat and a hard-hat. The bison nodded and then pushed the buffalos roughly along the path, deeper into the town.

"I wonder where they're going," McMoo muttered.

As the ter-moo-nator walked back inside the "monster", Bo suddenly noticed scraps of grey cloth flapping around his horns. "Hey, Professor, he must be that ter-moo-nator we saw with Big-Pants in Dodgem – the robobozo who got those undies stuck on his head!"

"Looks like he's the driving force of the operation," McMoo observed as the flap closed up in the cow-carrier and it reversed away back down the road. "See? He's driving his 'monster' away again, ready to pick up the few remaining cows still roaming the plains."

A thought occurred to Bo. "Hey, do you think Madame Milkbelly's great-great-great-whatever-grandmother is down here?"

"Could be," McMoo agreed. "Let's hope nothing has happened to her – because if it has, that means Madame M. herself will never be born, the future will change and everything will end in disaster!"

"It's really comforting, having you around, Professor," Bo muttered. "I wish Cod's famous gunslinging mates were down here with us."

"Cod?!" McMoo took a deep breath.

"Bo, do you keep getting Lobster's name wrong just to annoy me?"

"Yep!" she admitted. "I'm only joking 'cos I'm worried. What do those Fed-up Bulls want with a load of un-clever Wild Western cows? Do you think they're trying to turn them evil and nasty, so they can build a mad cow army?"

"The F.B.I. has tried schemes like that before . . ." McMoo frowned. "But why would it want its army of cows to live like humans?"

Bo shrugged and sighed.

McMoo patted her comfortingly on the shoulder. "Come on. Let's mosey on down there and see, shall we?" He smiled. "Or do I mean moo-sey?"

Together, they picked a careful path down the steep cavern walls and jumped onto a dusty pathway that led to the main road. The village cows didn't notice them – they were too busy tending their gardens, sweeping their floors or clearing cowpats from their bathrooms.

McMoo and Bo hurried along the

main road, tracking the newly arrived
buffalos. They saw that the bison in the
hard-hat had crowded the cattle into
a paddock filled with timber and tools.
Scurrying for the cover of a big bale
of hay, the C.I.A. agents spied on the
gathering.

"Right then, you new recruits!" the
bison bellowed. "My name's Boss Byron.

You will find life very different down here. No more roaming the plains for you lot – oh no. Down here you must build your own home, and live in it too!"

Bo and McMoo frowned, and the buffalos swapped puzzled looks.

"Don't give me those big cow eyes," boomed Boss Byron. "You may not like the idea, but you had better get used to it!" He crossed to his pile of planks. "It is vital you learn how to build your own houses. Soon you will be moo-ving back above ground. And all cows – and

any calves they might have — must build identical houses all over the western plains . . ."

"I've heard of cowboy builders, but this is ridiculous," muttered McMoo. But then he gasped. "Oh no! Hang on a second . . ."

"What is it?" Bo hissed.

"I know what's going on!" The professor looked wild-eyed. "That bison builder, this underground village, training the cows to live in human houses — it's all part of the same brilliant plan!"

Bo put a hoof over his mouth. "Keep your voice down, Professor!"

"Don't be a spoilsport, Bo Vine," came a familiar mechanical voice behind them. "The professor may praise the F.B.I. as loudly as he likes!"

McMoo and Bo spun round to find T-65 had sneaked up behind them. As ever, Big-Pants Barmer was by his side.

"I'm glad you two weren't blown to bits in that there storehouse up above," growled Big-Pants, holding a stick of dynamite between her fat finger and thumb. Now I can finish the job down here – in person!"

Chapter Ten

TRAPPED!

"Not you two again!" McMoo groaned. "You keep turning up like bad pennies."

"Never mind the pennies," growled Big-Pants, waggling her stick of dynamite. "Where's my twenty thousand dollars?"

Bo blew a gum-bubble at her. "Hurt us and you'll never find out!"

"Hey!" Boss Byron strode crossly up to Big-Pants and the ter-moo-nator. "I'm trying to hold a class here, T-65. What's going on?"

"I'll tell you exactly what's going on!" McMoo jumped in. "In 1862, a special law called the Homestead Act was passed by Abraham Lincoln, the

American president." He turned to Bo. "I told you about it when we first met Old Josh, remember?"

"Sort of," said Bo. "It sounded well boring!"

"That boring law could mean the end of history as we know it," said McMoo gravely. "With so much land in the Wild West up for grabs, the Homestead Act gave it away for free — to anyone who built a house on Wild Western soil and lived in it for a length of time."

"Correct," said the ter-moo-nator coldly.

"Yes, sir-ee!" Big-Pants chuckled. "These cows are being trained to live like humans so they can take over the rest of the Wild West!"

"It's diabolical!" McMoo marched up to the ter-moo-nator in a fury. "You used your 'monster' to drive away the cowboys so you could take their land."

He rounded on Big-Pants. "And you've been taking *more* land from the likes of Lobster Lobo by cheating at cards!"

T-65 nodded his metal head in agreement. "Meantime we have mined out this entire area to build our underground village," he said. "And we are using the precious metals we have mined to buy even more of the land above . . ."

"But it's dumb!" said Bo flatly. "Cows can't live in houses in the nineteenth century. No one will take them seriously."

"Oh, but they will," said T-65, smiling. "Because F.B.I. agents with ringblenders will pose as American politicians. Once elected, they will clear the way for cows to buy their own land – so we won't need people like Big-Pants Barmer to buy it for us."

"You heard him, Big-Pants – the F.B.I. is using you!" cried McMoo. "The moment you're no good to them any more, they will ter-moo-nate you."

"Maybe." Big-Pants shrugged. "But with the money they're paying me, I'll take my chances!"

"Think of it, Professor," grated T-65. "Within ten years, cows will own whole American states — Utah, Kansas, Colorado . . ."

Boss Byron the bison nodded. "Forget the free cow country of Luckyburger, nearly seven hundred years in the future," he said. "We're starting *Lasso*burger right here, right now!"

"And, in secret, we shall train the entire cow population into a savage fighting force," said T-65, "ready for the day they overthrow the entire USA!"

McMoo clapped a hoof to his forehead. "A nation of killer cows in the heart of the most powerful nation in the world!"

Bo pulled a face. "That's not good."

"And it's especially not good for you two." Big-Pants waved her stick of dynamite in the professor's face. "Now unless you want me to light this and shove it somewhere nasty, TELL ME WHERE MY MONEY'S GONE!"

"All right, then," said the professor. He quickly pointed behind her. "It's over there."

"Where?" demanded Big-Pants, turning in surprise . . .

Just as Bo leaped into action! She struck Big-Pants in the belly with a kung-moo chop. The gargantuan gunslinger fell to the ground, and the shockwaves nearly knocked T-65 off his hooves.

At the same time, McMoo grabbed
Boss Byron's hard-hat and flipped it
onto the ter-moo-nator's snout. It got
stuck there, the yellow rim blocking his
robotic vision. "Emergency!" cried T-65,
flailing about blindly. Bo grabbed Boss
Byron by the hoof and swung him
round into the ter-moo-nator. Both
went down with a colossal crash.

"Run!" McMoo shouted, and he
charged away down the path with Bo
at his side.

"I can't believe Big-Pants fell for the old 'It's behind you' number," panted Bo. "That's got to be the oldest trick in the book!"

"Ah, but it's 1875, remember?" McMoo smiled. "So that particular trick is a bit younger than in our own time."

"There is no escape from the F.B.I., McMoo!" came T-65's electronic roar behind them. He was already back up on his hooves and chasing after them. Big-Pants and Boss Byron were limping along after him, their faces twisted in rage . . .

"It's OK," said Bo, forcing herself to run faster. "They'll never catch us up."

But then a laser blast shot over their heads!

"They don't need to catch us up!" McMoo shouted. "This part of the path is dead straight – so T-65's got a clear shot at us. There's nothing in his way!"

But for about the first time ever, Professor McMoo was actually proved wrong. Because the next moment, there was something in T-65's way! A huge black-and-white cow wandered out in front of the ter-moo-nator, a group of young calves right behind her. They blocked the road completely!

"Stand aside!" shouted T-65 crossly.

But the mother cow seemed scared. She reared up and knocked the ray gun from T-65's metal hoof!

"You clumsy cow!" cried Big-Pants. But as she stooped to grab the gun, two of the calves dropped massive cowpats right on top of it! "Ughhhhh," the gunslinger groaned. "Who's got a glove?"

Still running onwards, Bo glanced back over her shoulder at the unexpected roadblock. The big black-and-white cow had an udder the size of an overweight collie – and was winking at Bo like she had meant to get in the ter-moo-nator's way all along . . .

"Professor!" Bo gasped. "We've been saved — by a cow who looks exactly like Madame Milkbelly!"

"Bless my horns!" said the professor, looking back to see for himself. "That must be Madame M.'s distant relative — alive and well and showing plenty of natural intelligence!"

But while Bo and McMoo were marvelling at the view behind them, they forgot to look where they were going. It took a familiar, ear-splitting roar to remind them of their mistake . . .

McMoo whirled round and skidded to a stop — and found himself blinded by the glare of headlights. "The Longhorn Monster!" he cried, grabbing Bo by the tail to stop her charging headlong into it. "Back already with a new cargo of cows!"

"Now you are finished!" shouted T-65. While Boss Byron shooed away the cattle on the road and Big-Pants rummaged in the muck for the gun, the ter-moo-nator was free to head straight for them. "I told you there was no escape!"

"Old metal-mush is right," said Bo as the glowing cow-carrier ground slowly towards them, closer and closer. "We can't go forward and we can't go back. We're trapped!"

Chapter Eleven

UNDERGROUND SHOOTOUT!

McMoo and Bo stared in dread as the huge "monster" spun round to present them with its luminous backside . . .

"There's nowhere to run, C.I.A. fools!" called T-65 as he clanked menacingly towards them. Big-Pants was trailing after him with the ray gun and dynamite clutched in her filthy hands. Boss Byron stalked beside her, holding a large shovel like a baseball bat.

As the loading flap began to open up in the cow-carrier's rear, Bo took McMoo's hoof. "Don't worry, Professor," she told him. "I'm here."

He smiled kindly. "Thanks, Bo. But I wish we were both somewhere else!"

The ramp clunked into place on the roadside . . .

And suddenly, two familiar figures burst from out of the monster's bottom!

"Pat!" McMoo was beaming from horn to horn. "And Lobster!"

"How'd you get inside the monster?" Bo asked in amazement.

"Remember those rustlers who nearly got us when we first arrived?" Pat pulled out a silver gun and pointed it at T-65 and his evil allies. "We saw that they'd caught some more cows, so we waited for the 'monster' to find them."

Lobster nodded. "And when it did, we overpowered ole Pants-Head the ter-moo-nator and got inside!"

"Attack!" roared T-65.

"I wouldn't if I were you," Pat shouted. "I've got your fellow ter-moo-nator's butter bazooka here, and I'm not afraid to use it!"

But T-65 ignored him. "TER-MOO-NATE THEM ALL!"

"Gimme that!" Bo snatched the weapon from Pat and opened fire, showering the F.B.I. assault force with a stream of stinky yellow sludge.

"Ugh!" shrieked Big-Pants as her clothes were soaked through with smelly, slippery spread. Her weapons flew into the air as she slid about and crashed into T-65. He, in turn, knocked against Boss Byron and they both fell into an enormous buttery puddle.

"Nice rescue." Bo passed the bazooka to Lobster and grabbed her brother in a hug. "But next time don't leave it so late!"

Pat grinned. "If it wasn't for the professor's micro-camera we wouldn't be

here at all. I took a picture when the
monster attacked us, and saw it was
running on wheels. That's when I
guessed it wasn't really eating the cows
– it was transporting them."

Suddenly T-65 jumped up and lunged
for his enemies with an angry electronic

screech. Lobster drove the ter-moo-nator back by spraying smelly butter up its mechanical snout.

But Boss Byron was already speaking into a radio. "Ha!" he laughed, pointing back down the road. "I just called for reinforcements. My guards will destroy you for this!"

McMoo gulped to see twenty F.B.I. troops – all without ringblenders – rampaging towards them.

"Luckily we've got back-up," said Pat coolly.

"Yeah, they're just breaking into the fancy weapons case in there . . ." Lobster turned back to the flap in the cow-carrier's backside. "Ain't you got them guns yet?" he hollered. "You're missing all the fun out here!"

A moment later, two tough-looking cowboys and a cowgirl rode down the ramp on horseback, holding more of the futuristic weapons. Despite their strange surroundings they looked as hard as stone, as cool as cacti and meaner than mosquitoes with machine-guns. Boss Byron's guards saw them too – and suddenly skidded to a stop, mooing uncertainly.

"It's . . . it's the Wild West legends!" breathed McMoo, awestruck despite the danger all around. "Buffalo Bill, Calamity Jane——"

"– and James the Jessie!" Bo declared. He scowled at her and she fluttered her eyelids: "Er, Jesse James, I mean."

"That's right!" Pat grinned. "We were down in Lobster's mine when we heard footsteps coming. We thought it was the F.B.I.——"

"But really it was my old gunslinging mates!" roared Lobster. "They *did* get my letter asking for help after all!"

"Attack them, you fools!" Boss Byron shouted feebly to his dithering guards. "You still outnumber them by more than two to one — you'll squash them!"

"We'll see about that," drawled Calamity Jane. "We found us a whole load of fancy weapons in the back of that monster-thang."

Buffalo Bill pulled out a chunky silver device. "This here's a sour-cream shotgun."

"And I've got a cream-cheese launcher!" said Jesse James proudly.

"Well, don't just stand there looking pretty, boys and girls," snarled Lobster as Boss Byron's guards started stampeding again. "Let's git firing and deal with these circus bull wannabes!"

"We're with ya, Lobster," bawled Buffalo Bill. "Yeee-hah!"

"Take cover, Bo!" cried Professor McMoo — as Lobster's outlaws opened fire on the approaching bulls. Sour cream went streaming through the air. Rancid butter shot out like water from a hose. Runny cheese, years past its sell-by date, spurted from the barrels of the

stolen guns. The bull guards were soon
skidding and slipping and gasping for
breath as a powerful pong filled the air.

"Yeee-hoooo!" yelled Calamity Jane.
"They're dropping like flies!"

McMoo beamed at Pat. "This really is a *legendary* rescue!"

"You did good, little bruv," Bo agreed. Then she saw one of the guards trying to crawl away, and gave him a serious squirt of milk, right between the eyes. "Fastest udder in the west!" she cried.

But with a sudden roar of anger, T-65 jumped up from his smelly puddle and hurled himself at Professor McMoo. "You will never defeat us!"

With a gasp, McMoo fell over – and then Big-Pants Barmer and Boss Byron slithered on top of him too . . .

"Don't shoot!" Pat told the outlaws. "You might hit the professor."

Bo was about to jump in and try to rescue him – when Lobster pulled her back. "Look out!" he yelled.

Suddenly Bo saw that a wooden barrel was hurtling down the steep rocky slope of the cavern wall, bouncing towards the bundle of bodies smothering

McMoo, faster and faster, until—
WHAMMMM!

With an echoing crash the barrel banged right into T-65's robotic bum.

"Urrrrk!" The ter-moo-nator was sent somersaulting over McMoo, sparks flying out of his butt as he knocked Big-Pants and Boss Byron aside. "Professor!" Pat gasped, helping McMoo to his hooves.

"Are you all right?" asked Bo.

"Oh, I'm having a barrel of fun!" McMoo smiled weakly and looked round at Big-Pants, Byron and the fallen F.B.I. agents, lying in a daze and splattered in gunk. "But at least I'm doing better than this lot!"

"Where did the barrel come from?" asked Lobster. He tapped the battered wood with his foot – and it groaned.

"Jumping Jiminy!" cried Calamity Jane. "There's something inside!"

"Hey," cried Bo as a familiar wrinkled face poked out into view. "It's Old Josh!"

"That was the rottenest dang journey of my whole life!" the old-timer complained, looking very wobbly as he climbed out of the barrel. "I hid in my barrel and got blasted all the way to the top of the hill – then I started rolling back down again . . ."

"And you fell through that hole in the ground we blew open!" McMoo realized. "Imagine that!"

"None of you will need to imagine it!" roared Big-Pants Barmer, struggling back up in a raging fury. "I'm gonna make another hole in the ground right here – and you'll all be buried in it!"

She held her stick of dynamite up to T-65's sparking bottom and lit the fuse. "Suck on this, you crummy critters!"

And she hurled the dynamite — straight at McMoo!

Chapter Twelve

THE GOOD, THE BAD
AND THE UDDERLY

"Look out!" boomed McMoo.

Pat braced himself as the stick of dynamite spun through the air like a sinister sparkler. Everything seemed to happen in slow motion.

Lobster and his gunslinger buddies hit the deck.

Bo grabbed Old Josh and crouched over him protectively.

Laughing like a drain, Big-Pants Barmer dived for cover behind the still-sparking ter-moo-nator.

And McMoo turned to Pat, his face never more serious. "I've always told you to use your head – don't let me down now!"

The sizzling stick of dynamite was mere millimetres away when the professor turned nimbly on one hoof and swatted it delicately with his tail. The gentle blow had changed the dynamite's course – and now it was heading

straight for Pat!

"The monster!" yelled McMoo. Pat gulped, held his breath and crossed his hooves all at once – and just managed to catch the dynamite with his horns.

In the same moment he flicked his head to the left and the dynamite went soaring through the air again.

And this time it shot straight into the hatch in the monster's bum!

Big-Pants spluttered with helpless rage. "Nooooooo!"

Then Pat saw no more as Professor McMoo flattened him against the floor.

Ka-VOOOOM! There was a mega-loud explosion that shook the whole cavern – but the monster contained the blast! It glowed dazzlingly bright for a moment. Smoke and steam belched out from the darkness inside.

Then the monster's headlights flickered on and off, its engines spluttered into life – and it moved jerkily towards them.

"Everyone up!" McMoo commanded, jumping to his hooves. The cow-carrier lurched to one side and smashed into the cavern wall. Then it reversed at high speed and nearly squashed Old Josh as it crashed into the wall opposite. The roof began to shake, and the sound of worried mooing soon carried from every house in the underground village.

"Alert!" A further crash jerked the very dented T-65 upright, still sparking all over. "The monster's drive systems have been damaged by the explosion — it is out of control!"

Suddenly the monster's horns shot off in a cloud of smoke, shooting through the air like javelins. They struck the cavern roof and hung there, as black jagged cracks stretched crazily across the rock. Then the malfunctioning monster drove off again, crashing through whole rows of the little underground houses. Cartloads of cattle fled in fear and confusion as the cow-carrier started demolishing the entire place.

Pat winced. "There goes the neighbourhood."

"You mean the *moo*-bourhood," said McMoo sadly, watching the concerned cows charge about.

"Not fair!" wailed Boss Byron, curled up in a buttery heap on the ground. Rubble fell from the roof and the mighty sun lamp in the ceiling began to flicker. "Everything's gone wrong!"

"I'm off!" Big-Pants announced, running for the nearest exit. "So long, suckers!"

"Let's get her!" Bo cried.

Pat shook his head. "We can't go, Bo – we're needed here."

"Indeed we are," McMoo agreed. "T-65, your plans are ruined. We must work together now to help these kidnapped cows back to the surface."

"Negative," groaned T-65, sliding a silver disc from under his battered breastplate. "A-a-a-a-bort. Mission a-a-a-abort!"

"No!" cried McMoo. But in a swirl of black smoke, the ter-moo-nator, Boss Byron and his dairy-dunked guards all faded away.

"Now I've seen everything!" Lobster declared.

"Wrong," said Bo. "You haven't seen us evacuate hundreds of cattle from a collapsing cave, have you?"

"But you will now," McMoo added. He turned to Lobster and the gunslingers. "Please – will you help us?"

"Sure!" Buffalo Bill grinned and jumped back onto his horse. "I once rounded up a thousand buffalo in a single day. How do you think I got my name?"

"And there's nothing Jane likes better than a calamity!" Calamity Jane declared.

"I've always liked cows," added Jesse James. "Especially roasted!"

"I'll pretend I didn't hear that," said Bo, scowling. "OK, let's moo-ve, everybody — before this whole cave comes crashing down around our ears!"

Swiftly, with skill and style, the Cows in Action took charge of the rescue mission.

The Wild West legends lived up to their reputations. They stayed cool, calm and capable in the crumbling cavern, rounding up the runaway cattle and steering them out of the various exits dotted around the underground village.

Pat and Bo, being cows themselves, were able to soothe the frightened herds as they helped them back up to the surface. They took extra-special care of the ones who had blocked T-65's way back on the road. The biggest, oldest cow smiled at Bo knowingly. There was no doubt in Bo's mind that this was Madame Milkbelly's distant relative.

"No harm's coming to her, or to the future," Bo declared. "Not with us around!"

And as the last cows were led away, McMoo finally managed to climb on board the out-of-control monster and deactivate it. As it ground to a halt, drained of all power, the professor stared round in wonder at the trail of destruction it had left in its wake.

Then the flickering mini-sun in the ceiling went out, plunging the gigantic cavern into cold darkness. The only remaining light came from the dying glow of the Longhorn Monster. But it was enough for McMoo to make his escape through a passageway close by – just as the cavern roof fell in.

McMoo ran on desperately, the ground shaking beneath his hooves as thousands and thousands of tons of rock crashed down on the secret cow community, burying every last trace of the F.B.I.'s fantastical plan.

He found his friends and the gunslingers waiting for him on the plain in warm sunshine, surrounded by grateful cattle as far as the eye could see.

"Professor!" Pat cried as he spied him. "You made it!"

Bo ran over and gave McMoo a huge hug. "Well done, Prof!"

Panting for breath, McMoo gave them a weary grin. "Well done to all of you too!"

"And especially to Old Josh," said Pat happily. "He's made the kidnapped cows an offer they can't refuse . . ."

Old Josh nodded. "I still got that twenty thousand dollars I won off Big-Pants," he said. "I reckon some of it should go into building a grand old cow sanctuary where these poor cows and their calves can live out the rest of their lives in peace and happiness."

McMoo beamed. "That's the most beautiful, *moo*-tiful thing I ever heard!"

Then Lobster Lobo stepped forward. "And to make sure Old Josh don't get no trouble, me and my gunslinging buddies are gonna take some garbage back to Dodgem . . ."

Buffalo Bill nodded and moved his

horse aside to reveal not only the rustlers Jim Bob and Henry tied up on the ground – but Big-Pants Barmer too!

McMoo stared. "Where did you find her?"

Bo sniggered. "She was too fat to fit through one of the exit tunnels, and got jammed there!"

Jesse James grinned. "We thought we would have to light more dynamite to blow her free . . ."

"But then your little friend came up and butted me in the butt!" Big-Pants complained, rubbing her behind.

"I sure did!" Bo giggled. "She popped out like a cork from a bottle!"

Lobster smiled. "Well, I reckon I'll be popping the cork on a bottle myself tonight – to celebrate getting my mine back!"

"Party time!" cried Calamity Jane.

"Yeee-hah!" whooped Buffalo Bill.

"Soon as people hear that the

monster's pushed off, and that they were tricked out of their land, they'll all be partying!" said Old Josh. "This whole area will start filling up fast again."

"Just as it was always meant to," said Pat quietly. "History is back on track."

"C'mon, guys," said Lobster to his gunslinging gang. "Let's take our prisoners over to the sheriff in Dodgem and start celebrating!"

"Have a lemonade for me, Lobster!" Bo shouted.

He frowned. "So you knew my name all along?"

"Course I did!" She grinned. "How could I forget a name like Lobster Oboe?"

"That's Lobo! Grrr . . ." Lobster pulled his hat down over his eyes and rode away. "GOODBYE!"

"So long, everybody!" McMoo watched Lobster and the Wild West legends as they rode away across the plains, towing Henry, Jim Bob and Big-Pants behind them. Soon they were just silhouettes against the clear blue sky.

Then they were gone.

"Time we were going too," said McMoo. He clapped Old Josh on the back and shook hooves with Madame Milkbelly's distant relative. "Enjoy your freedom," he said.

The grand old cow simply winked and nodded.

Then McMoo, Pat and Bo headed back to the Time Shed.

The walk took the C.I.A. agents several hours and a couple of wrong turnings. But the journey back to their farm in the Time Shed took no time at all.

"Home again, in our own time," said McMoo. "Get the tea on, Pat!"

Pat crossed to the kettle – then froze as the sound of distant, tuneless singing floated through the shed's doors. "That's Bessie Barmer!" he realized, frowning in alarm. "I'd forgotten – she's struck gold, remember? She's going to sell the farm!"

Bo sighed and nodded. "Maybe we should head back to Old Josh's cow sanctuary!"

"No need," came a gruff voice – as Director Yak breezed inside the Time Shed.

"Yakky baby!" cried Bo, running up and planting a big lipsticky kiss on his nose. "What are you doing here?"

Yak rubbed his snout and tried not to blush. "I'm escorting *her*," he explained, pointing behind him – to where Madame Milkbelly stood smiling!

McMoo and Pat got down on their knees, and Bo attempted a clumsy curtsey.

"Oh, please get up!" said Madame Milkbelly. "I simply wanted to congratulate you all in person for a job well done – and for saving my ancient ancestor."

"It was an honour," McMoo assured her.

"She was cool," Bo enthused. "In a sort of wrinkly old cow kind of way!"

"Shut up, Bo!" hissed Pat.

"Plus we knew you were worried about Bessie selling the farm," Yak added quickly. "So I checked my twenty-first-century history books and came to tell you the good news . . ."

Madame Milkbelly nodded. "Bessie Barmer hasn't struck gold at all."

"She hasn't?" Pat blinked. "But . . . I saw something gleaming in her hand."

"Don't sweat, trooper." Yak tossed a shiny lump of metal over to McMoo. "It was just a lump of this stuff."

The professor caught it, studied it – and smiled. "This is iron pyrite," he announced.

Bo sniffed. "Iron what?"

"Pyrite," the professor repeated. "It looks a bit like gold, but it isn't. It's known more commonly as . . . fool's gold!"

"Oh, what a shame!" Pat grinned. "When she finds out—"

"AAAUUUUGHHHHH!" came a distant, dismal shriek.

"I think she just found out!" Bo chuckled. "Fool's gold is right — there's no bigger fool than Bessie!"

"In every sense," McMoo agreed. "Looks like the farm is safe after all."

"And so is the future," said Madame Milkbelly. "Thanks to each of you."

"I'll drink to that!" cried Pat, cracking open a fresh box of tea bags.

"And I'll drink to more mega-exciting missions," Bo added.

Yak smiled. "I'm sure you've got many more to look forward to."

"So am I," said McMoo happily. "Because when it comes to mega-exciting missions — no matter where or when we end up — the C.I.A. strike gold every time!"

THE END

IT'S 'UDDER' MADNESS!

Genius cow Professor McMoo and his trusty sidekicks, Pat and Bo, are star agents of the C.I.A. – short for COWS IN ACTION! They travel through time, fighting evil bulls from the future and keeping history on the right track ...

When Professor McMoo invents a brilliant TIME MACHINE, he and his friends are soon attacked by a terrifying TER-MOO-NATOR — a deadly robo-cow who wants to mess with the past and change the future! And that's only the start of an incredible ADVENTURE that takes McMoo, Pat and Bo from a cow paradise in the future to the SCARY dungeons of King Henry VIII ...

It's time for action.

COW-ER WITH FEAR!

Genius cow Professor McMoo and his trusty sidekicks, Pat and Bo, are star agents of the C.I.A. – short for COWS IN ACTION! They travel through time, fighting evil bulls from the future and keeping history on the right track . . .

In ANCIENT EGYPT, a monstrous *moo-my* has come to life and kicked the PHARAOH off his throne. Sent to investigate, the C.I.A. agents face PERIL in the pyramids and nightmares on the Nile. Can they foil a TERRIFYING time-crime before the whole WORLD falls to the moo-my's curse?

It's time for action.

WHERE NO COW HAS GONE BEEF-ORE...

Genius cow Professor McMoo and his trusty sidekicks, Pat and Bo, are star agents of the C.I.A. – short for COWS IN ACTION! They travel through time, fighting evil bulls from the future and keeping history on the right track ...

The C.I.A. travel back to the ROMAN EMPIRE, where TER-MOO-NATORS are turning innocent bulls into WARRIORS! With all Rome at risk, McMoo, Pat and Bo battle GLADIATORS and race to the death in CHARIOTS, trying to solve a moo-stery that could wreck history FOR EVER!

It's time for action.

Collect them all!

Riddle of the Raptors

The Hatching Horror

The Seas of Doom

The Mind-swap Menace

The Skies of Fear

The Space Ghosts

Day of the Dino-Droids

The Terror-Bird Trap

The Planet of Peril

Teeth of the T. rex

The Star Pirates

www.astrosaurs.co.uk